The Ballet Slippers

The Ballet Slippers

Written by

Melony Bates

Illustrations by

Amy Sunluvr

Blue Cove Publishing/Dunnellon FL

Melony Bates/Blue Cove Publishing
P O Box 1828
Dunnellon, Florida 34430

www.melonybates.com

www.bluecovepublishing.com

Publisher's Note: This is a work of fiction. Names, characters, places, and incidents are a product of the author's imagination. Locales and public names are sometimes used for atmospheric purposes. Any resemblance to actual people, living or dead, or to businesses, companies, events, institutions, or locales is completely coincidental.

Cover Art by **Anastasia Yatsunenko**

Book design © 2013 BookDesignTemplates.com

The Ballet Slippers/Melony Bates — First Edition

ISBN 978-1-945595-01-1

First Printing in the United States of America

For HIM,

-above all.

Chapter 1

"Have a good weekend, Megan," the school bus driver said.

"Bye, Mrs. Hutchison!" Megan yelled back as she leaped off the bus. She completely missed the bottom step and landed on the ground with both feet. She ran straight inside the front door of her family's rented house, letting the old rusty screen door slam behind her. She dropped her book bag and jacket on the floor by the front door.

"Guess what, Guess what, Guess what?" she said, her voice full of excitement as she ran into the living room where her family was sitting.

"What, What, What?" Dad asked.

"We had a show today at school from a real dance studio," Megan said. "They did ballet, that's where the dancers dance on their toes. Like this!"

She raised her arms over her head forming a circle and tried to stand on the tips of her toes and spin around.

"They wore ballet slippers. They were pink and shiny and they had pink ribbon ties that laced up around their ankles. The ballet slippers help them stay up on their toes when they dance. And they danced like this." Megan explained as she tried again to imitate the ballet dancers from the performance. "If I had a pair of those ballet slippers I could stand on my toes and I would just dance and dance and dance."

"That must have been something to see," Grandma said, as she looked up from her crochet. "I always thought ballet was pretty too. I never got to see it though, except on TV, but I always thought it was pretty."

"I bet that was really something to see," her dad said. "But ballet slippers probably cost a lot of money and I'm sure the dance lessons probably do too."

"I don't need lessons," Megan said shaking her head. "I don't. My friends, Jasmine and Ashley, are going to take lessons. They already signed up, and they said that I could go with them and watch them take their lessons at the dance studio and then we could all practice together later. I just need some ballet slippers so I can practice with them."

"I wish you could have a pair of those ballet slippers, but we just can't afford anything extra right now, Meggie," Dad told her.

"I'm sorry sweetheart, money is just really tight right now," Mom added.

"I know...I just wanted to tell you about them," she answered and slowly walked back to the front door to pick up her jacket and book bag. Megan knew money was tight. It was always tight and she knew her mom and dad did the best they could for her and her grandmother. So she never asked for anything unless she really needed it.

I know Mom and Dad can't afford to buy me a pair of ballet slippers right now, Megan thought as she walked upstairs to her bedroom. And I don't want to make them feel bad, but I really want them. I want them more than I have ever wanted anything else, she said to herself as she pretended to be a ballet dancer in front of her bedroom mirror. I have to find a way to get them. I just have to.

No matter how hard Megan tried, she couldn't stop thinking about the ballet dancers wearing those pretty, pink ballet slippers with the ribbon ties.

I need a pair of those ballet slippers. There has to be a way to get them, she thought. She wanted them so bad it seem to hurt deep inside her.

That night, Megan said her prayers and got into bed. She tried to go to sleep but her eyes just wouldn't stay shut. All she could do was toss and turn, and think about the ballet slippers.

When she finally lay still for a moment, an idea popped into her head. Mom and Dad work hard every day for what we buy. I could work too! I could get some kind of job. I can do things, she thought. Maybe I could work for the neighbors and save up the money to buy a pair of ballet slippers for myself.

She tried again and again to go to sleep, but couldn't. Her mind was just too busy. She began to plan how she would work and who she could work for. She would save up for her ballet slippers a little at a time until she had enough money to buy them. Then she could go watch Jasmine and Ashley take their dance lessons, and then they could all practice together later. She would dance and dance and dance. She would spin around on her toes just like the ballet dancers she had seen at the school performance.

But first, in the morning, she would have to ask her mom and dad if she could.

Chapter 2

The next morning was Saturday. She would be able to get started working as soon as Mom and Dad gave her permission.

She got up early and was dressed and sitting at the table in the kitchen before Mom and Grandma had to call her to eat breakfast.

"Good morning, Sweetie," Grandma said as she looked up from the stove where she was cooking. "You're up and dressed early for a Saturday."

"Good Morning, Sweetheart," Mom said as she set the plates and forks on the table.

"Good Morning," Megan said, anxiously waiting for everyone to sit down.

Dad came in, kissed her on the top of the head and tousled her hair with his fingers before sitting down at the table. "Morning, Meggie," he said.

"Good morning, Daddy," she cheerfully answered.

Grandma was a wonderful cook. She made pancakes and homemade syrup every Saturday morning and they all sat down and ate breakfast together.

"After breakfast, can I go out and ask the neighbors if I can do some stuff for them to earn some extra money?' she asked before shoveling a piece of syrup drenched pancake into her mouth, dribbling a little syrup onto her chin. "I want to save up and buy a pair of ballet slippers." She said wiping the sticky off her chin.

Dad smiled and said, "I guess that will be alright, as long as you have your room cleaned, your homework done, and Mom and Grandma don't need you around here."

"They're both done. Mom? Grandma?" she asked.

"Sure, go ahead, but finish your breakfast first. Remember to ask nicely and do a good job!" Mom said.

"Always say 'Thank You', dear," Grandma added.

"I will," she assured them and gobbled down the rest of her breakfast.

Megan skipped down the sidewalk of her street. Maple Street felt like her street. She had lived there her whole life. It was in the old part of town with old houses and mostly only older people lived there. She was the only kid who lived on Maple Street. The only other time she saw other kids there were when they came to visit their grandparents, usually on weekends and holidays.

The first neighbor she came upon was Mr. Wilson. He was sitting on the big gray stone steps that led up into his house and leaning back on the porch handrail.

He was a nice old man who used to be a schoolteacher, but had long since retired. His wife had died many years ago and he lived alone now. He walked with a cane and he had little clear plastic tubes in his nose to help him breath. The tubes ran down into an oxygen tank that he rolled along beside him wherever he went.

"Well hello Megan?" Mr. Wilson said as she walked up the sidewalk toward him. "How are you this morning?"

"I'm doing great! How are you today?" she asked.

"Oh, doing pretty well for an old man my age, I guess," he replied.

"Mr. Wilson, do you have any small jobs I could do to earn some extra money?" she asked.

"What do you need money for child?" he asked.

"I'm going to buy a pair of ballet slippers!" she answered.

"Ballet slippers?" he asked.

"Yes, and I'm going to dance just like the real ballet dancers, on my toes...like this!" She raised her hands above her head and tried to stand on the tip of her toes and spin around to show him.

"You look like you'll be pretty good at it," he said with a smile. "Well, let me see."

Megan looked down and kicked around some of the fallen leaves that were piling up on the ground.

"How about raking the leaves in your whole yard?" she asked.

"I don't know, Megan. It's a pretty big yard. There's a lot of leaves. It might be too big of a job for an eight-year-old," he told her.

"I can do it, Mr. Wilson," she said trying her hardest to convince him. "I can do it. And I'll do a really good job."

"Well...OK, you can try it. Come on and I'll show you where the rake and the bags are," he said as he slowly got up from the stone steps, dragging his oxygen tank behind him.

Chapter 3

At first, the rake, with its long wooden handle seemed big and awkward to Megan. She conked herself on the head a few times before getting the hang of it. She was determined that she could do it and she could do a good job. Most of all, she wanted to make the money to save for her ballet slippers.

Mr. Wilson sure does have a lot of trees, she thought as she looked around at the job she had just taken on. She raked and raked. She filled bag after bag and there was still a lot of yard left and a lot of leaves to rake.

Mr. Wilson was right, it was a big yard, much bigger than it had looked when she had asked to rake it. She felt tired but she knew she couldn't give up, no matter how big the job was. She wanted those ballet slippers more than anything.

She passed the time by daydreaming about getting her pretty, pink ballet slippers and floating on her toes just like the real ballet dancers.

She had just finished raking up a huge pile of leaves when she began to feel a little burning spot on both of her hands. She stopped and pulled off the gloves Mr. Wilson had given her to wear. They were his wife's old gardening gloves, and were way too big for her hands but Megan made them work the best she could. She could see the red spots where a couple of blisters were forming on her hands.

"Ouch!" she said as she rubbed the sore spots.

"Yahooooo!" She heard a voice yell and it was coming toward her fast.

"No! Stop! Don't!" she shouted as she looked up and saw a boy running.

He jumped right on top of the huge pile of leaves she had just finished raking. The leaves scattered everywhere and there was absolutely no pile left.

"What are you doing?" she scolded the boy as the leaves that went up in the air floated slowly down past her face.

"Jumping in a big pile of leaves!" the boy answered as he got up and dusted the leaves out of his hair and off his clothes. "That's what you do with a big pile of leaves. That was great!"

"Not if you're trying to rake them up to put into bags!" she snapped.

"Why would you want to do that with a perfectly good pile of leaves? Are you being punished or something?" he asked.

"I'm working for extra money to save up for something?" she said. Megan started raking up the leaves again, forgetting about the blisters on her hands.

"You have to work for the things you want?" the boy asked looking puzzled.

"No, I just want to!" she answered.

"My mom and dad buy me whatever I want. I don't have to work for anything. All I have to do is ask for it and they get it for me," he told her.

"So!" she shrugged. Megan was used to her friends and other kids having more than she did. She never had the newest games or toys and her clothes didn't come from fancy stores. Even the furniture in her bedroom didn't match. But Grandma made most of her clothes so she always had something nice to wear. And she knew her mom and dad worked very hard just to get by and did the best that they could. She knew they would get her extra stuff if they could.

"What are you working to buy anyway?" the boy asked.

"Don't worry about it!" she snapped back, clearly annoyed that he had even asked and not wanting to tell him anything.

"No, really, what are you going to buy?" he asked again.

"Ballet slippers!" she said wishing right away that she hadn't told him.

"Ballet slippers? Are you serious?" the boy sneered. "What do you want with a pair of them sissy dance shoes anyway? I'd buy me something really fun like a skateboard or a scooter!"

"That's what I want, so just don't worry about it!" she told him. She sighed and went back to raking up the pile of leaves again. She ignored him hoping he would leave. "Stupid boys!" she mumbled as soon as he left. "I don't care if he does get anything he wants."

Finally, she finished raking the leaves and filling the last bag in Mr. Wilson's yard. It took her all day Saturday and three days after school to rake and bag all those leaves in his huge yard. It took a lot of big black plastic bags to hold all those leaves. He paid her ten dollars.

"Wow! Thank you so much, Mr. Wilson!" she said as she looked at her first earnings.

"Well, it was a lot of work, and you did a good job, Megan. I hope it helps you get those dancing shoes you want," he told her.

"It will," she said.

Megan ran all the way home with her money tight in her hands and straight upstairs to her room. She jumped up on her bed and stared at her ten-dollar bill. It was the first money she had ever earned. It was the first money that was ever really her very own. She could do whatever she wanted to with it. And she knew exactly what she wanted to do with it.

"Ten whole dollars!" she said to herself. "Now I need something to put my money in." She looked around her room for something to hold her first earnings. "I need a big jar or something to keep my money in."

She went downstairs to the kitchen and looked under the sink. She knew Grandma always kept old jars and stuff under there.

Grandma always told her, "Never get rid of something you might need later."

She found a large empty pickle jar that would be just right.

"Grandma, can I have this old pickle jar to put my money in?" she asked holding it up for Grandma to see.

"Yes, you can have that one," Grandma answered. "That one will sure hold a lot of money."

"Thanks, Grandma," Megan said.

She ran back upstairs and put her ten-dollar bill in the big glass jar. She sat it on her dresser so she could see it even from her bed.

"Tomorrow I have to find another job so I can make some more money to fill up that big jar," she said. She smiled, proudly admiring her first earnings.

Chapter 4

Mrs. Parsons, who lived a few houses down from Mr. Wilson, was in her front yard kneeling down working in her flower garden.

Megan was a little afraid to approach her because she seemed a little cranky every time Megan had tried to say hello to her before.

"Mrs. Parsons?" she asked timidly.

"Yes!" Mrs. Parsons snapped from beneath her big straw gardening hat.

"Hi, I'm Megan. I live right up there and...," she stopped when Mrs. Parsons interrupted her.

"Are you selling something? Well, if you are, I don't want it!" she snapped and went back to her gardening.

"No, ma'am, I...well, I'm trying to earn some extra money and I was wondering if you had any jobs I could do," she asked.

Mrs. Parsons turned her head and peered up at her from under her big straw hat.

"Well, I could use some help pulling weeds out of my gardens. My back just isn't what it used to be. But you're going to have work hard and I don't want to hear any complaining!" she snapped with her scratchy old voice.

"No, ma'am, I won't complain and I will work hard" Megan promised.

"Alright, let's go get you some gloves," Mrs. Parsons answered as she slowly got up from her knees off the ground. "You can't do decent gardening without a good pair of gloves."

After Mrs. Parsons found a pair of gloves for Megan, she began to show her what she wanted done.

"This is a weed!" Mrs. Parsons spouted as she pointed to the plants. "This is not a weed! These are my flowers, so don't pull them up!"

"Yes, ma'am," Megan answered. She was very careful what plants she pulled up and which ones she did not. If she wasn't sure she would ask. She did not want to upset Mrs. Parsons. She was grouchy enough without anyone upsetting her.

Mrs. Parsons worked right beside her all afternoon without saying much, except when it came time for Megan to leave.

"You have a lot to learn but you did okay today." Mrs. Parsons said as she handed Megan a couple dollar bills. I'll need you here tomorrow afternoon for my fall vegetable garden. Don't be late or I'll just do it myself!"

"Thank you, Mrs. Parsons. I'll be here right after school," Megan said, feeling a little stiffness in her back from pulling weeds all afternoon. She suddenly understood why Mrs. Parsons grunted a little when she stood up and stretched out her back.

"Wow! Two more dollars to add to my pickle jar, that's twelve whole dollars now. I'll have my ballet slippers really soon," she said to herself.

The next day, right after school and after a quick snack of milk and warm ginger snap cookies that Grandma had made for her, she was out the door and back down the street at Mrs. Parsons' house as she promised.

Mrs. Parsons was just as grouchy as the day before and they got right down to work weeding the vegetable garden.

"This is a weed! This is not a weed! These are my vegetables, so don't pull these up!" Mrs. Parsons instructed Megan again.

"Yes, ma'am," Megan answered timidly. She was never sure if Mrs. Parsons was mad at her or just mad at the world, but either way it made her nervous.

"Do you like vegetables?" Mrs. Parsons asked.

"Yes, ma'am," Megan answered, but remembered she really didn't like squash, "Well, most of them anyway."

"Which ones don't you like?" Mrs. Parsons asked sternly. "I like them all.

They are all good for you. I don't know why anybody wouldn't like any of them."

"Just squash," Megan answered.

"There's nothing wrong with squash!" Mrs. Parsons sharply informed her.

"I know, but I like everything else," Megan answered.

"Well, that's good. Most kids these days don't want to eat anything that's good for them, just pizza and junk food!" Mrs. Parsons rattled on.

"I don't. I've only had pizza a few times at my friend's house. My grandma cooks everything we eat at home. She's a really good cook," Megan told her.

"Yes, I know your grandmother, Virginia. She is a good cook. She sent me some bread she baked and a jar of her peach jam a while back. Your father brought them over."

Mrs. Parsons' voice seemed to soften and become a little nicer as she spoke of Grandma's kindness.

"Well, looks like we're about done here. It looks good. You did okay today, too. Here's a couple of dollars for today."

"Thank you, Mrs. Parsons," Megan answered with a big smile on her face, and started to run home.

"Are you coming back tomorrow?" Mrs. Parsons called to her.

Megan stopped and turned around. "Do you have some more work I can do tomorrow?"

"Tomorrow is Saturday; I have several things I want to get done. I have to trim these shrubs," Mrs. Parsons said pointing to the bushes in front of her porch. "You can pick up the clippings. That will take most of the day."

"Yes ma'am. I'll be here right after breakfast," Megan answered.

"Don't be late or I'll just do it myself!" Mrs. Parsons spouted.

"I won't, I'll be here. Thanks, Mrs. Parsons," Megan called back as she started again for home.

Another two dollars to put in my pickle jar, she thought as she counted her money in her head. Fourteen whole dollars now! It was really starting to add up. Soon she would have her pretty, pink ballet slippers.

Chapter 5

Megan worked most of the day on Saturday with Mrs. Parsons, picking up shrub clippings and pulling vines that had grown through and around some of the shrubs.

This time when they finished all that work, Mrs. Parsons paid her five dollars.

"Thank you so much," Megan said as she took the money.

"What are you going to do with all that money?" Mrs. Parsons questioned. "You're not going to just go throw it away on some worthless junk, are you?

Most people have no idea how to manage money anymore!"

"I'm saving for a pair of ballet slippers. My friends are taking ballet lessons and I want to learn to dance too," she explained.

"Are you going to take lessons? You need lessons, you know, if you are going to learn to dance properly," Mrs. Parsons informed her.

"No ma'am...I can't take lessons right now," Megan explained. "But I'm going to go watch my friends take lessons and then we are going to practice together later."

"Well, that's alright. Sometimes you do what you have to," Mrs. Parsons said. "That's good of your friend's though."

"Yes, ma'am, Ashley and Jasmine have been my best friends since kindergarten. We do everything together," she replied.

"You can come by every once and a while, you know, to see if I need you for something." Mrs. Parsons said sounding a bit lonely.

"I will. Thank you." Megan said. She couldn't help feeling a little sad for Mrs. Parsons. Maybe she wasn't just grouchy. Maybe she was really lonely and just acted grouchy to cover it up.

Megan walked home instead of running. She was really tired. It was hard working and saving for something that she really wanted. But she knew it would all be worth it when she finally had her pretty, pink ballet slippers.

"Now I'll have nineteen dollars in my jar! I can't wait until I have enough. I can't wait until I can go and buy my ballet slippers," she said. "Tomorrow is Sunday so I won't be able to work. But, after church and lunch I can rest."

On Monday afternoon, she changed out of her school clothes and went to get a snack before heading out to earn more money.

"Hi Grandma," Megan said.

"Hi Sweetie," Grandma answered but not in her normal cheerful way.

Megan noticed her grandma wrapped up in a quilt and holding a tissue.

"Grandma, what's wrong?" she asked.

"Oh, just an old cold I can't seem to get rid of. Don't worry, I'll be okay," Grandma answered.

Grandma doesn't look well at all, Megan thought. Her face seemed pale and she looked very tired. "Do you need me to stay home to take care of you this afternoon, Grandma?" she asked.

"No, that's very sweet dear, but I'm just going to stay here and rest. Your mother took me to the doctor today and got me some more medicine. It will start working soon. She had to go back to work, but she'll be back in a little while. Can you get your own snack today or do you need me to get it for you?" Grandma asked.

"No, I can get it Grandma," Megan answered. "You stay there and rest. I'll just be down the street if you need me."

"Okay dear," Grandma answered and then drifted off to sleep in her favorite old chair.

Megan looked back at her grandma before going out. She suddenly felt bad for not noticing that Grandma was sick before now. She had been so wrapped up in earning money that she hadn't really thought about much else.

Chapter 6

Megan could see her neighbor, Mr. Gonzalez, working inside his open garage. She knew most everybody on Maple Street and they knew her so it was always easy to find someone to talk to, even if they were all grownups.

"Hi Mr. Gonzalez," Megan said as she walked up his driveway.

"Hi Megan," he said as he looked up from his project.

Almost every time she saw Mr. Gonzalez, he was tinkering in his garage with something. Other times she would see him and Mrs. Gonzalez out walking their two little house dogs.

"What are you working on?" Megan asked.

"Just this old waffle iron. It has a short in it or something. Probably just need to buy a new one, but maybe I can fix it. I don't know, but we'll see," he said with a grin on his face. "What are you up to this afternoon, little one?"

"I was wondering if you had any jobs I could do. I'm trying to earn some extra money," she told him.

"Oh, you are, are you?" he asked jokingly.

"Yes sir," she answered.

"Well, let me see. Can you fix this old waffle iron?" he teased.

"No sir, but I can do other stuff," she told him.

"Well, let me see. Hmm, can you sweep out this garage?" he asked.

"Yes sir," she said smiling.

"Well, there's the broom and the dust pan. And you're sure you can't fix this old waffle iron for me?" he joked.

"No sir, I don't think so," Megan said as she began sweeping the garage floor, trying not to cause too much dust.

But Mr. Gonzalez began to pretend to be choking.

"Sure is getting dusty in here," he said grabbing his throat and still pretending to cough. "I can't breathe!"

"Mr. Gonzalez, stop it. You're not choking, you're just teasing me," she said laughing at him.

"Okay, I'll behave," he said, but every time she looked up he pretended to grab his throat and cough. He was so funny she was having a lot of fun doing this job.

When she finished sweeping up the garage, Mr. Gonzalez reached in his pocket and gave her all the change he had.

"Now that you're finished, I can go back to breathing in here," he teased.

"Thank you, Mr. Gonzalez," she said holding both her hands together to hold all the coins he had just given her. "Do you have any other jobs I could do?"

"Well...I still have this old waffle iron. You're sure you can't fix this for me?" he joked.

"Mr. Gonzalez!" she said laughing. He was so funny.

"Well, come back tomorrow. I'll ask Mrs. Gonzalez and see if we can come up with some small jobs for you to do," he told her.

"I'll come back tomorrow right after school," she assured him.

"Okay, see you tomorrow, Dusty!" he teased.

"Mr. Gonzalez, that's not my name," she said.

"I think I'll start calling you that anyway," he said laughing.

"Mr. Gonzalez!" she said and she waved goodbye.

When Megan got home, she went straight upstairs and dropped the handful of change into the big glass pickle jar. She didn't have time to count it before she heard her mother call her.

"Megan!" Mom called. "Can you come downstairs and set the table for me?"

"Yes ma'am," Megan answered. "I'll be right there." Grandma must be really sick if Mom is cooking supper by herself, she thought. They always cooked supper together.

"Grandma isn't feeling well tonight," Mom said.

"Is she going to be alright?" Megan asked.

"I think so. The doctor gave her some stronger medicine. I went to the drug store right away and picked it up so she could get started taking it. She should start feeling better soon," Mom assured her.

"I hope so," Megan said.

"Me too," Mom agreed.

Chapter 7

Mr. Gonzalez was in his garage tinkering around with that old waffle iron again when Megan arrived.

"Have you fixed it yet?" Megan asked.

"No, but I think I have almost got it," he said with a smile. "What are you up to today?"

"Remember I asked you yesterday if you had any jobs I can do to earn some extra money," she reminded him.

"Hmm. Let me think. Are you sure you asked me? It might have just been someone who looked like me?" he teased her.

"Mr. Gonzalez!" Megan said.

"No, I'm just kidding. I remember. I spoke to Mrs. Gonzalez and she says she can find some things for you to do today. She's inside," he told her pointing at the back door with a screwdriver.

Megan laughed and went inside to speak with Mrs. Gonzalez.

"Hi, come on in Megan," Mrs. Gonzalez said.

"Hi," Megan answered.

As soon as she got all the way in the door, the Gonzalez's two little dogs came running at her, barking and all excited, jumping up and scratching her legs threw her jeans with their little sharp toenails.

"Ouch!" Megan said as she rubbed her legs.

"Get down! Get down you two!" Mrs. Gonzalez scolded the little dogs. "Mr. Gonzalez said you want to do some things to earn extra money?" she asked.

"Yes ma'am," Megan answered.

"Well, I have a few things that need to be done if you would like to do them," she told Megan. "But some of them are not very fun to do."

"That's okay, I won't mind doing them," Megan assured her.

"Well okay then, the first job is cleaning up the back yard where the dogs play," she said as she pointed out the big sliding glass doors to their fenced in back yard.

"Okay," Megan answered, "I can do that."

Mrs. Gonzalez handed her a small plastic scoop and a plastic bag.

"Put all the doggie poop in this bag and then tie it off. If you need another one just let me know. Pick up all of their toys and put them in the plastic storage box on the porch," Mrs. Gonzalez instructed.

Megan looked at the scoop and the plastic bag. She slowly walked out the big glass doors to begin cleaning up the Gonzalez's back yard. She wrinkled up her nose as she thought about scooping up dog poop. She thought about going home, but she remembered how much she wanted a pair of those pretty, pink ballet slippers with the ribbon ties.

"Ewww!" Megan said as she scooped up the little piles of dog poop and put them carefully in the plastic bag, closing it quickly each time trying not to smell it.

"Yuck! Dogs are so nasty," she said to herself. "Thank goodness they are little dogs or I would have to have a lot more bags!"

"How are you coming with the backyard?" Mrs. Gonzalez stuck her head out the glass doors to ask.

"Just fine, Mrs. Gonzalez," Megan answered trying to smile. "But I will be glad to be done with this job!" she mumbled to herself after Mrs. Gonzalez closed the door. She continued to scoop up all the piles of dog poop and picked up all the dog toys in the Gonzalez's back yard until the job was finished.

"You did a good job, Megan. Here's a couple dollars," Mrs. Gonzalez praised her as she handed her the money.

"Thank you." Megan answered politely. But she thought to herself, this was an awfully nasty job for only two dollars?

As she walked home she counted up the money in her head. "Wow! Twenty-one dollars and some change now, I think." she said. "That's still not enough to get my ballet slippers. I have to find something else to do tomorrow."

Chapter 8

Megan had finished all the bigger jobs she could find to do in her neighborhood. Now, all she could find were really small jobs, the ones that didn't take very long to do. None of them paid more than whatever spare change her neighbors had in their pockets or had lying around. Her savings were not adding up very fast now, but at least they were still adding up.

She swept off porches and sidewalks. She brought in the neighbor's mail. She helped walk the Gonzalez's little dogs, which was much more fun than scooping up their stinky little poop. She did not volunteer to do that job again.

The afternoon before trash pickup, she took everyone's trash to the curb. She collected a lot of change on trash day.

Whatever anyone would let her do, she did it. But it took a lot longer for the change to add up to much.

"Did you get your ballet slippers yet?" all the neighbors would ask when they saw her or passed her on the street.

"No, not yet," she would answer, "but I almost have enough."

"You'll get them. Keep up the good work," they all would encourage.

"I will," she would say. She knew she just needed a little more and then she would have them. She was very close.

Tomorrow was Saturday again and she would work all day if she could find some jobs to do.

By Saturday afternoon, when she had collected the money on her last job for the day, she again counted her earnings in her head. She was sure she finally had enough to buy her ballet slippers. She

didn't walk home today, even though she
was tired. She ran.

Chapter 9

"Hey wait," a voice called from behind her as she was running home.

Megan knew exactly who that voice belonged to. She did not want to stop and talk to him. Oh great, it's that stupid boy again! Good thing I'm not raking leaves, she thought as she tried to ignore him and continued to head home to count her money.

"Did you get enough money to get your ballet slippers yet?" the boy asked as he tried to catch up with her.

"I think so!" she yelled without looking back.

"Great!" she heard him call from behind her.

In her room, Megan poured all the money out of the big glass pickle jar onto her bed. She carefully recounted her money.

Finally, she had enough to buy a pair of ballet slippers.

She jumped up and ran downstairs to ask her mom and dad if they would take her to town next Saturday to get them. It was a whole week until then and waiting would be the worst thing.

When she reached the bottom of the stairs, she could hear her mom and dad talking in the kitchen. When she got closer, it sounded like they were talking about something serious. Megan wasn't sure if she should interrupt them or not. She stopped in the hallway and listened.

She heard her dad say, "Grandma's doctor bills and her medicine really took a chunk out of our paychecks this week. I just don't see how we're going to be able to pay the rent on the house this month. I think we can make all the other bills, but there just isn't enough left for the rent."

Megan knew her Grandmother had been really sick but she didn't realize that her doctor bills and her medicine had been so expensive.

She heard Dad say, "If we could just come up with a little more we could make the rent payment."

It made Megan feel sad that her parents had to worry so much about money when they both worked so hard.

"I really don't know where we're going to come up with anymore," her mom said sounding worried. "Where are we going to move if we lose this house?"

We're going to have to move? Megan thought sinking back against the wall. But we've always lived here.

"I'll go talk to Mrs. Sawyer in the morning. I don't think she will throw us out. We've never been late before," Dad said.

Megan slowly walked back upstairs, no longer thinking about the ballet slippers she wanted so badly. All she could think about now was what she had overheard her parents talking about. She wondered how she could help as she sat on the edge of her bed. She looked over at the big glass pickle jar lying on its side and the money scattered on her bed.

"How can I buy ballet slippers for me when Mom and Dad need that money to pay the rent?" Megan asked herself. She grabbed the big glass jar, scooped up all of her saved money, and she took it downstairs.

She sat the big glass jar on the kitchen table in front of her mom and dad where they were still sitting and talking.

"Hi Sweetheart," Mom said looking very worried.

"Here's the money I saved. You can use this to help pay the rent," she told them.

Tears began to run down her mom's cheeks. "Megan...this is your money. You have worked so hard and saved this money for a pair of ballet slippers."

"I know...but you and Daddy work very hard too. And I want to help," Megan explained.

Mom pulled Megan to her, hugged her tightly and kissed her. Dad joined in and put his arms around both of them and kissed Megan on the top of the head, then he tousled her hair with his fingers.

The money that Megan had saved was just enough to add to what they already had to make the rent for the month.

"Thanks, Meggie," her dad said. "That was a very unselfish thing to do. This money will really help."

Chapter 10

The next Saturday morning came; the day Megan was supposed to go buy her ballet slippers.

She got up and got dressed just like she had on all the other Saturday mornings. She sat on her bed and looked over at the empty glass pickle jar sitting on her dresser. Megan remembered how hard she had worked and how long it took to earn that money. She sighed deeply as she thought about it.

I'm glad I helped my family out with the house rent, but I wish I could have bought my ballet slippers with that money, Megan thought. I still want a pair of ballet slippers. Mom and Dad will never have enough extra money to buy them for me. I know that working and saving for them is the only way I'm going to get them, she reasoned with herself. I guess I better get started. So she rushed downstairs and ate breakfast so she could get started all over again.

Megan hurried out the front door of their rented house, letting the old rusty screen door slam behind her. She almost ran into their mailman, Mr. Davidson, on her way out.

"Well hello Megan!" the Mailman greeted her.

"Hi, Mr. Davidson," she answered as she rushed past him.

"Where are you going in such a hurry this morning?" He asked, "I have something for you."

"For me?" she asked stopping on the bottom porch step.

"I think so. It has your name on it," he told her.

"Really!" she asked.

"Yes, it says your name right here," he said pointing to the address label. "See, it says Megan on Maple Street. That's you," he said as he handed her the package.

"Thank you, Mr. Davidson," she said as she took the package inside. "Mom, Dad! Look I got a package!" Megan said excitedly. "See it's got my name on it. I never got a package before."

"You did?" Dad asked, "Who's it from?"

"I don't know. It just has my name on it," Megan explained as she began to rip off the brown paper that covered a box.

She opened the box slowly and then laid back the white tissue paper that was covering what was inside.

"Oh my gosh! Oh my gosh!" She shouted not believing her eyes.

"What is it, Sweetheart?" Mom asked.

Megan held the box up, inside was a pair of pretty, pink ballet slippers with pink ribbon ties just like the ones she wanted. Just like the ones she had been working and saving for.

"Where did they come from?" Mom asked looking over at Megan's dad.

Dad just shrugged his shoulders. "There's no return address," he said picking up the brown paper that Megan had torn off the outside of the package and let fall to the floor. "That's strange. I wonder why someone would not put a return address on a package."

Megan carefully pulled the ballet slippers out of the box and held them up, as she did a small white card fell to the floor. Dad picked up the card.

"Who's it from?" Mom asked.

"What does is say, Daddy?" Megan asked.

Dad just stared at the card for a moment and then smiled. "Here Megan, you read it," he said as he handed her the card.

The card had no name on it, only a few typed words in the center.

Megan smiled as she read the words on the card.

"To a kind and thoughtful little girl."

81

ABOUT THE AUTHOR

Melony Bates is an author of both fiction and non-fiction for children, teens and adults. She spent her early career in banking but her love for writing won and she is now enjoying writing full time.

Ms. Bates grew up in a large family, on a small farm in central Florida. She still lives in Florida with her husband. Her grown children and lots of extended family live nearby.

Watch for new books coming out soon.

www.melonybates.com

Made in the USA
Middletown, DE
14 October 2016